Experience the Color and Culture of Puerto Rico!

Enjoy!
Marisa de Jesús Paolicelli

Marisa de Jesús Paolicelli
Children's Author

"When Carlito the Coquí isn't Singing,
He's READING!"

Chi Chi Rodriguez
B o o k s

A gift from
Marlene (Linny) Fowler

The Beginning

There's a Coqui in My Shoe!

© 2003 text by Marisa de Jesús Paolicelli
Watercolor illustrations © 2007 Chi Chi Rodriguez Books

Published by Chi Chi Rodriguez Books

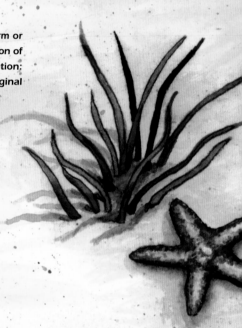

Second Chi Chi Rodriguez Books Edition, December 2008.
Printed in Malaysia

Editorial Director: Adolfo R. López
Consulting Editor: Dorothy Hoffman
Art Director and Title Design: Marisa de Jesús Paolicelli

Library of Congress Control Number: 2007905221

ISBN: 978-0-9797641-0-3

Tanja Bauerle's original illustrations were done in watercolor with prisma color detail on Arches watercolor paper.

Text Placement: Stacy Fiske, Graphic Artist/Design*Design*, Inc.

SUMMARY: A small boy discovers Puerto Rico's beloved amphibian, the *Eleutherodactylus coqui*, in his shoe, resulting in an everlasting friendship, and together they experience the wonders and beauty of the island.

There's a Coquí in My Shoe!

Story by Marisa de Jesús Paolicelli
Pictures & Cover Art by Tanja Bauerle

Chi Chi Rodriguez
B o o k s

I dedicate this book to Dr. Rafael L. Joglar,
Professor and Researcher, of the University of Puerto Rico,
for his life's work on researching the 17 species
of coquí frogs. Thank you, Dr. Joglar!

Marisa

"*You* consider yourself successful when you have helped a child take your spot when you leave this earth. If the kids succeed, the future is bright!"

Chuli

Chi Chi Rodriguez Books
Publisher of *There's a Coquí in My Shoe!*

Hidden Objects

There are <u>7</u> little coquíes, <u>17</u> piragüas (snow cones), <u>3</u> dominoes, <u>2</u> ducks, <u>1</u> golf ball, <u>1</u> cowbell, and <u>1</u> coconut hidden throughout the story. Can you help Humberto the Hummingbird find them all?

Armando was restless this evening, tossing and turning in his bunk bed. Usually by 9:00 p.m., he was sound asleep. Not even the steady patter of raindrops outside his bedroom window or the soft humming of his ceiling fan could help him drift off to the Land of Nod.

Armando was eager for tomorrow to arrive. Saturday was an important day for him and his mother, Lola —— the day they would open for business selling piragüas (pee-rah-gwas) in Old San Juan, Puerto Rico. Piragüas are snow cones and Armando and his mother had many flavors to choose from: pineapple parade, lemon lime, coconut kiss, tamarind hug, mango tango, raspberry blast, grape ape, and tropical blend.

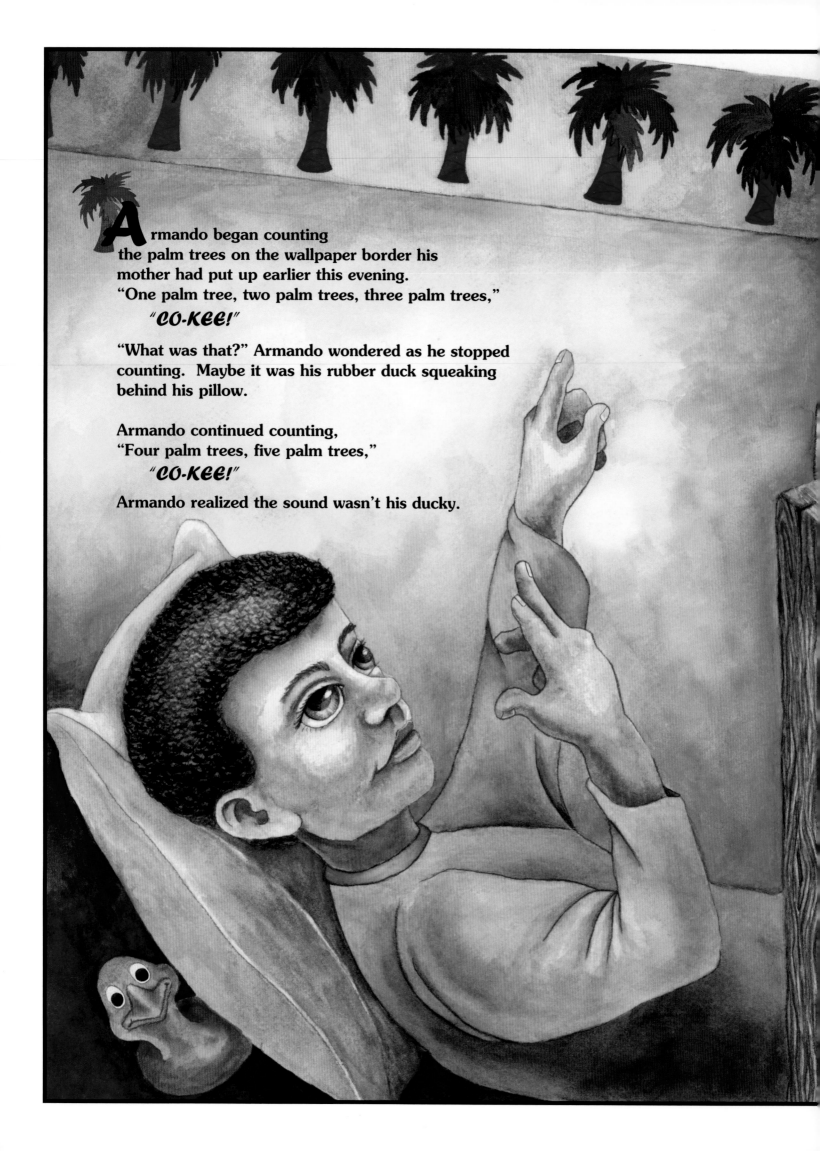

Armando began counting the palm trees on the wallpaper border his mother had put up earlier this evening.
"One palm tree, two palm trees, three palm trees,"
    "CO-KEE!"

"What was that?" Armando wondered as he stopped counting. Maybe it was his rubber duck squeaking behind his pillow.

Armando continued counting,
"Four palm trees, five palm trees,"
    "CO-KEE!"

Armando realized the sound wasn't his ducky.

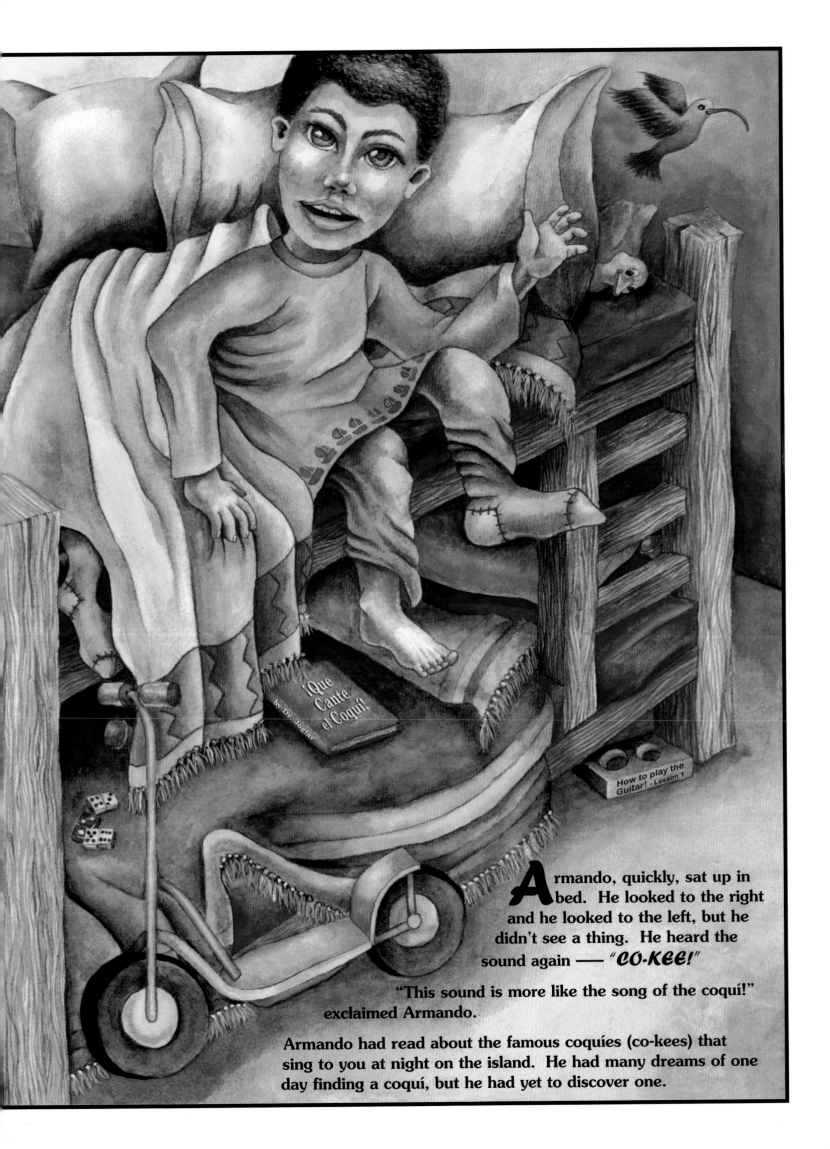

Armando, quickly, sat up in bed. He looked to the right and he looked to the left, but he didn't see a thing. He heard the sound again —— *"CO-KEE!"*

"This sound is more like the song of the coquí!" exclaimed Armando.

Armando had read about the famous coquíes (co-kees) that sing to you at night on the island. He had many dreams of one day finding a coquí, but he had yet to discover one.

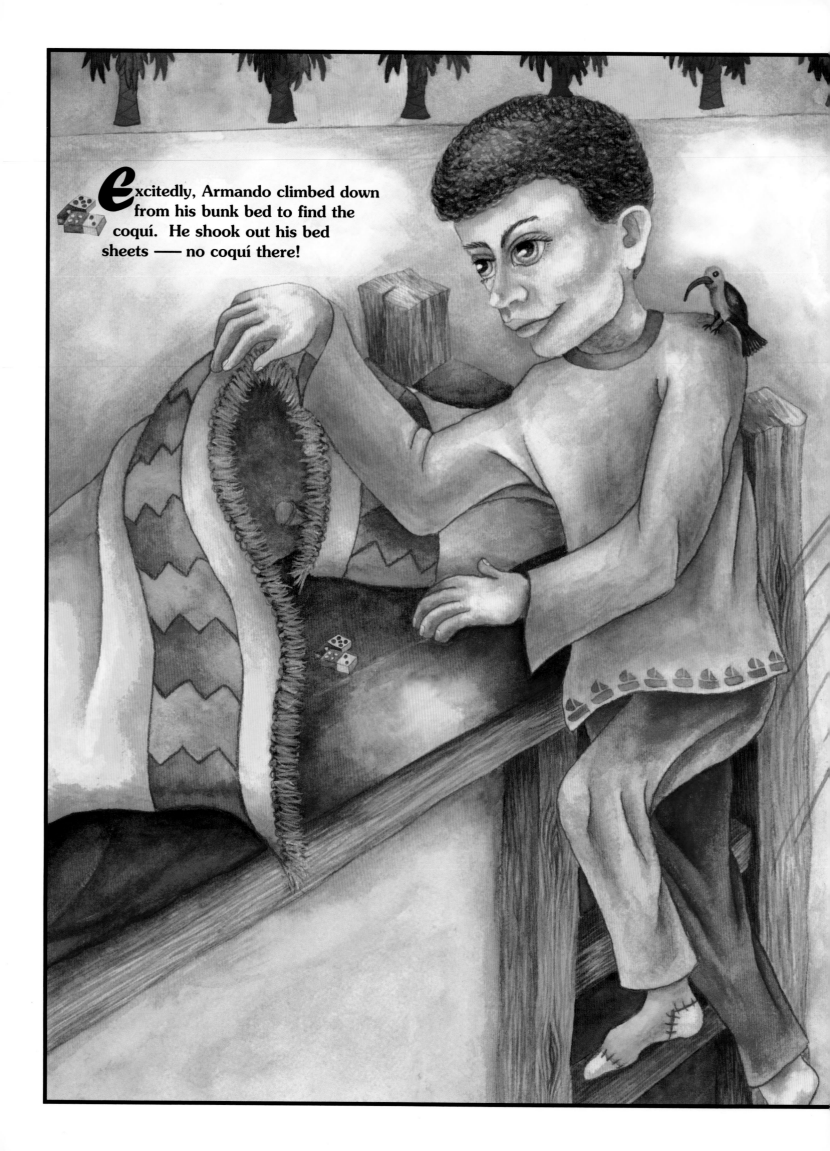

*e*xcitedly, Armando climbed down from his bunk bed to find the coquí. He shook out his bed sheets — no coquí there!

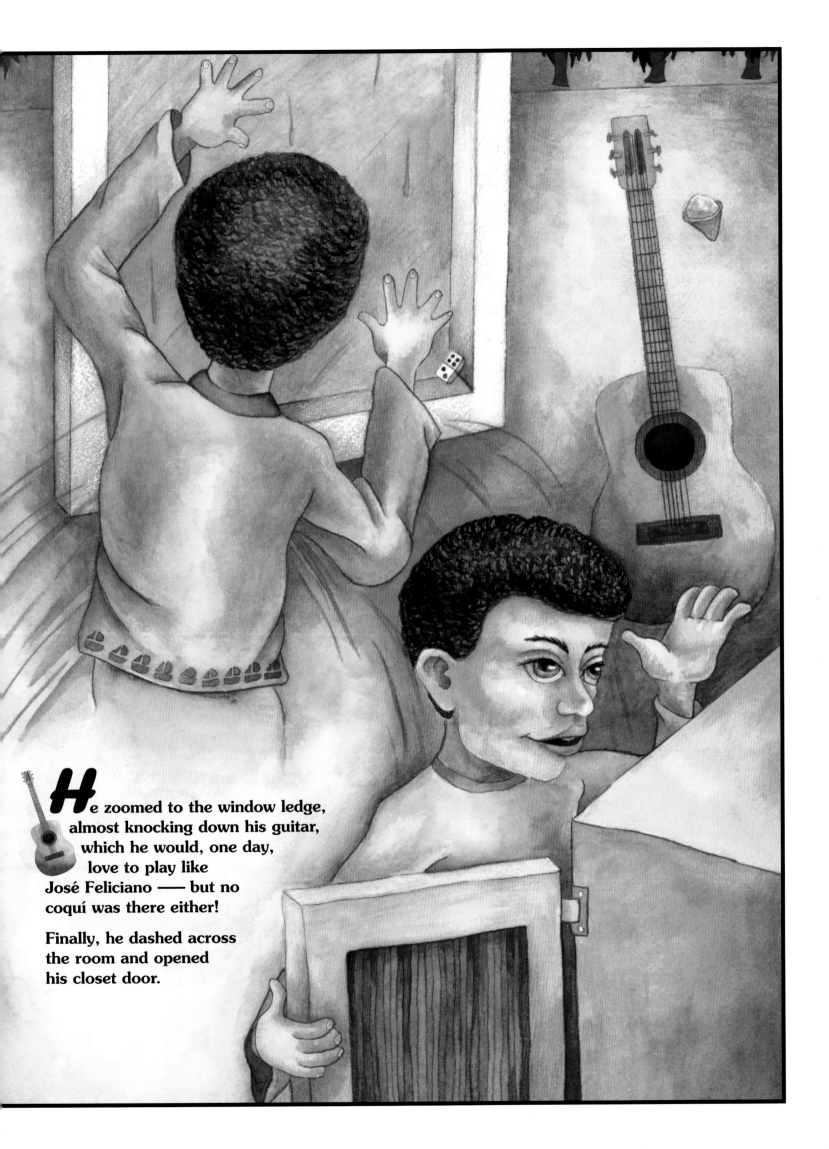

He zoomed to the window ledge, almost knocking down his guitar, which he would, one day, love to play like José Feliciano —— but no coquí was there either!

Finally, he dashed across the room and opened his closet door.

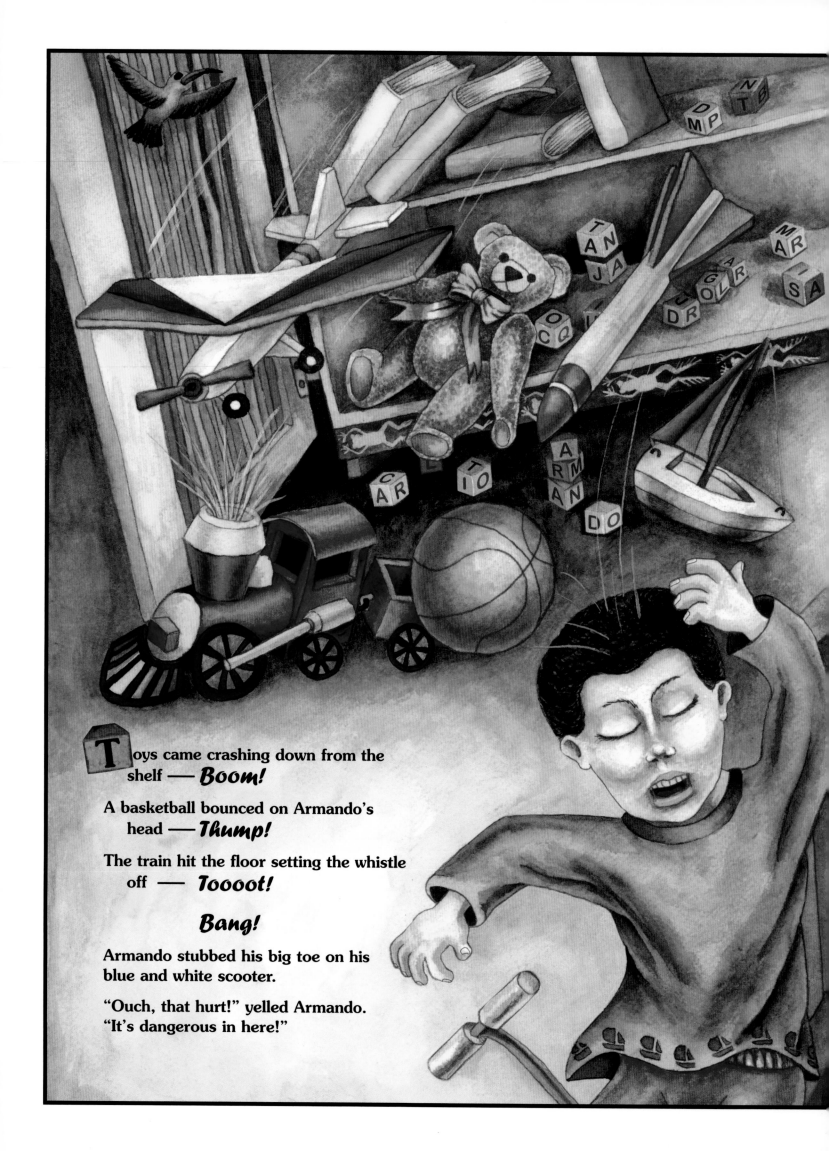

Toys came crashing down from the shelf — *Boom!*

A basketball bounced on Armando's head — *Thump!*

The train hit the floor setting the whistle off — *Toooot!*

Bang!

Armando stubbed his big toe on his blue and white scooter.

"Ouch, that hurt!" yelled Armando. "It's dangerous in here!"

SOFRITO

"Armando, it's getting late. Please get to bed," said his mother from the kitchen below as she placed the labels on the flavored syrups.

ouder and louder was the high-pitched
"*co-kee.*" Armando was getting closer.

Tucked away in a corner near his yellow tricycle, Armando
noticed his red shoes. The shoelace on one of them
wiggled like a worm.

"Ah, ha!" he cried out.
Curious, Armando slowly peeked inside the shoe and in a
blink of his eye . . .

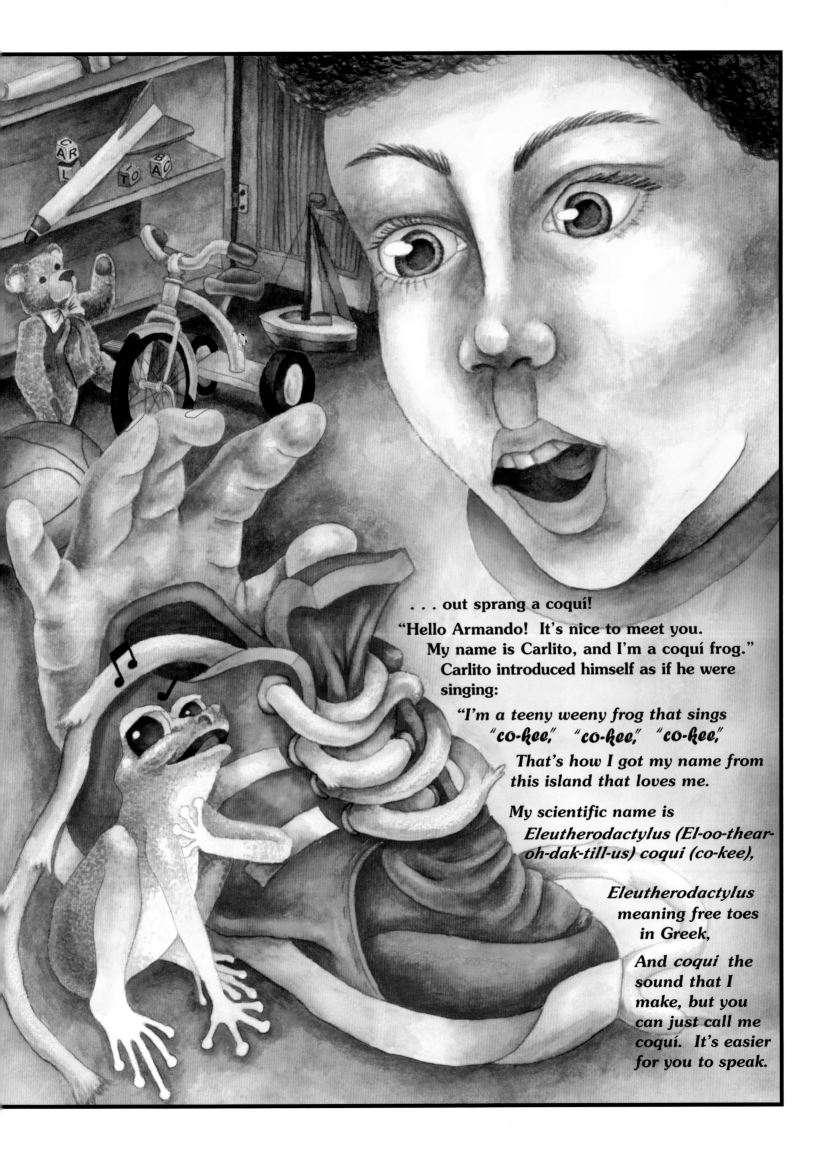

. . . out sprang a coquí!

"Hello Armando! It's nice to meet you. My name is Carlito, and I'm a coquí frog." Carlito introduced himself as if he were singing:

"I'm a teeny weeny frog that sings
"co-kee," "co-kee," "co-kee,"
That's how I got my name from this island that loves me.

My scientific name is Eleutherodactylus (El-oo-thear-oh-dak-till-us) coqui (co-kee),

Eleutherodactylus meaning free toes in Greek,

And coqui the sound that I make, but you can just call me coquí. It's easier for you to speak.

I cling to the leaves with the pads on my toes,
Webbed feet I don't have so swimming's a no.
I'm about the size of a dime or even a penny,
Eight or nine of us in your shoe is simply too many.

I live in El Yunque, a lush tropical rain forest,
A Puerto Rican tree frog I am, and now your best guest.

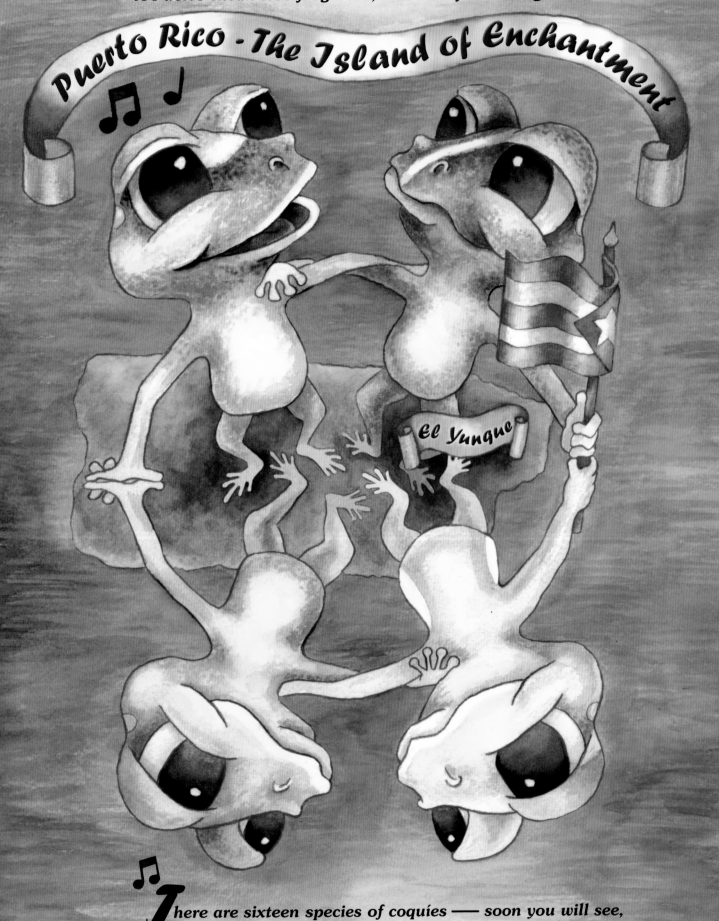

Puerto Rico - The Island of Enchantment

El Yunque

There are sixteen species of coquies — soon you will see,
Plus my species here, that'll be seventeen.
God made us with special marks and colors,
But in His great wisdom He decided not all green.

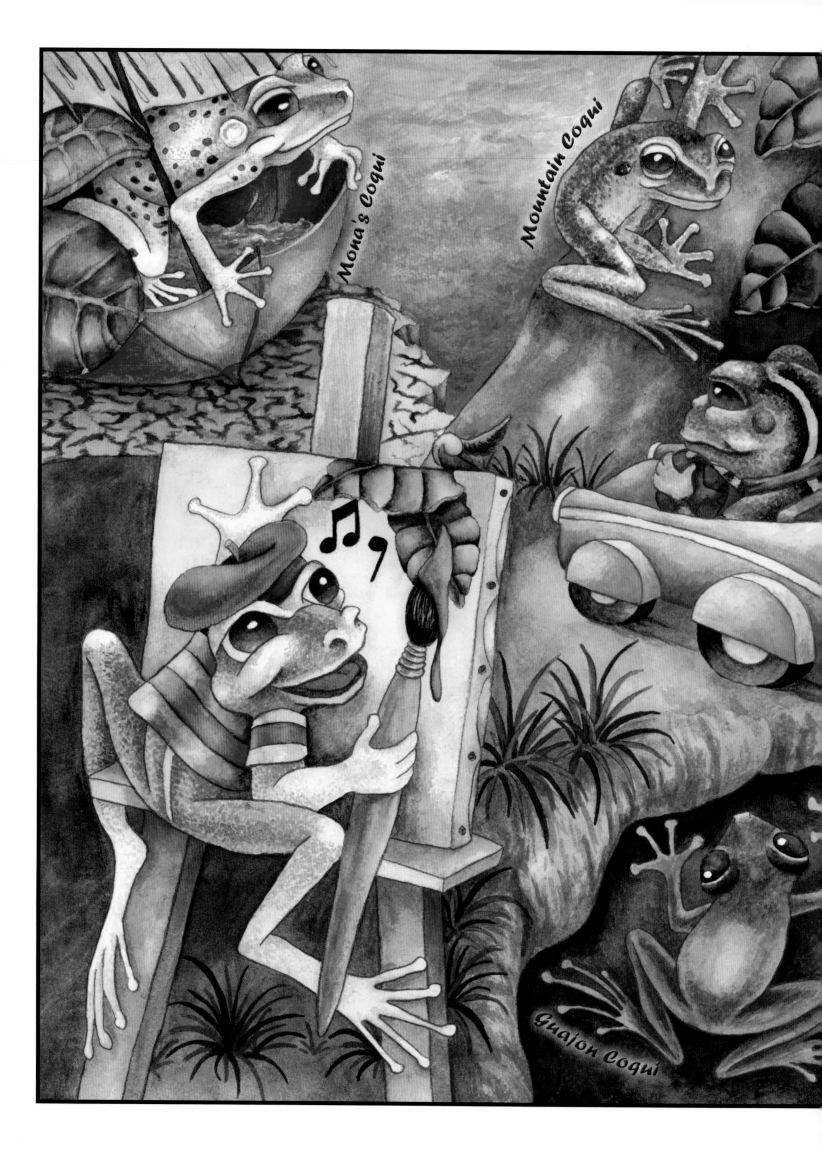

Some in my family live in the
highlands, lowlands, and dry places,
On the shores, in bromeliads (broh-meel-ee-ads –
native tropical plants) and mountain ranges.
Some lay their eggs in tree trunk holes being arboreal (ahr-bor-ee-al),
While others live on the ground being terrestrial (te-res-tree-el).
Some live on the island of Mona, out of sight most of the year,
Only to step out during the rainy season for
a breath of fresh air.
Some in my family have stripes down their backs,
Like racing cars *Vrooooom! Vrooooom!* Stopping at
your feet to say ¡Hola!
Some have huge eyes and long, long legs,
hiding in cracks and
living in caves.

Cricket Coquí

Golden Coquí

¡Hola!

Hedrick's Coquí

Webbed Coquí

Melodious Coquí

Like me, some have a broad band on the top of their heads,
    While many have stripes down their sides,
And we sing all night long until our mommies say *"time for bed."*
    Some in my family are gold, brown, and a bit gray,
Greenish-yellowish, black or spotty and we're all here to stay.
Some have punctuation marks on their backs, an inverted parentheses,
While others have no markings at all but are still some of the prettiest.

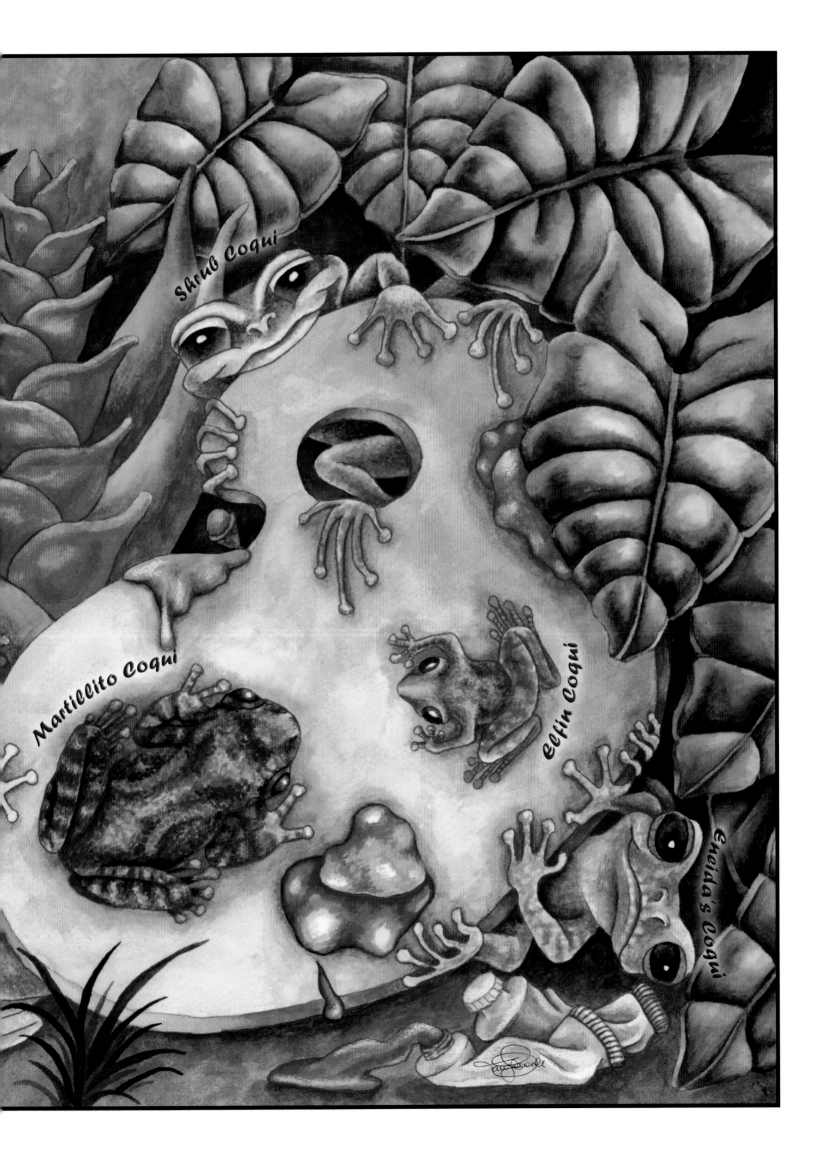

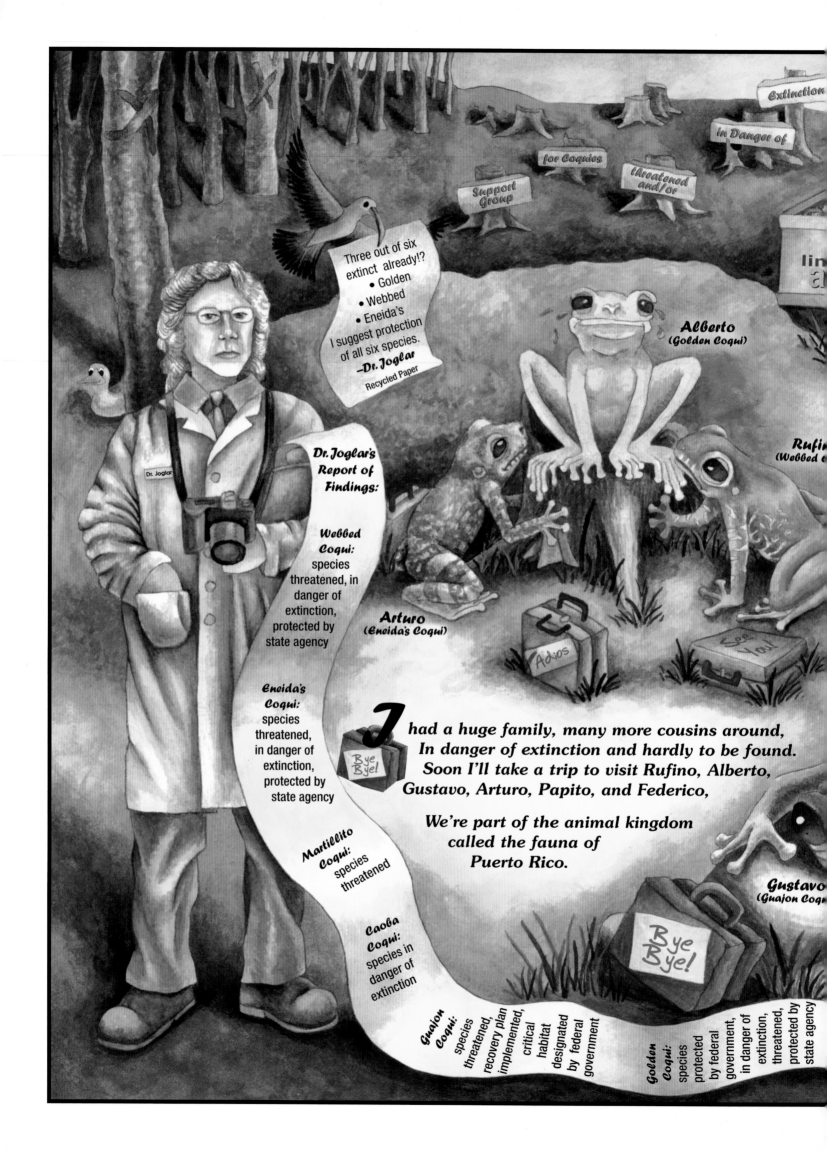

Sea Without Barriers Program

To the white, sandy beaches
    I sometimes jump, skip, and hop,
And play ball with the children
    while we drink guava punch.
Slurp, slurp, we're done
    but please, don't litter!
To keep clean all the beaches
    for you, me, and visitors.

Luquillo Beach

Tourism Company of Puerto Rico

I'm a national symbol,
here in Old San Juan,
Tied to their culture and
considered as one.
Next to their flag and
national flower,
"co-kee" I sing in
El Morro,
the tower.

"**A**s evening draws nigh in this Caribbean Paradise,
    I grace my sweet melody throughout the countryside.
Leading an orchestra for all to hear,
This is my home that I cherish both far and near."

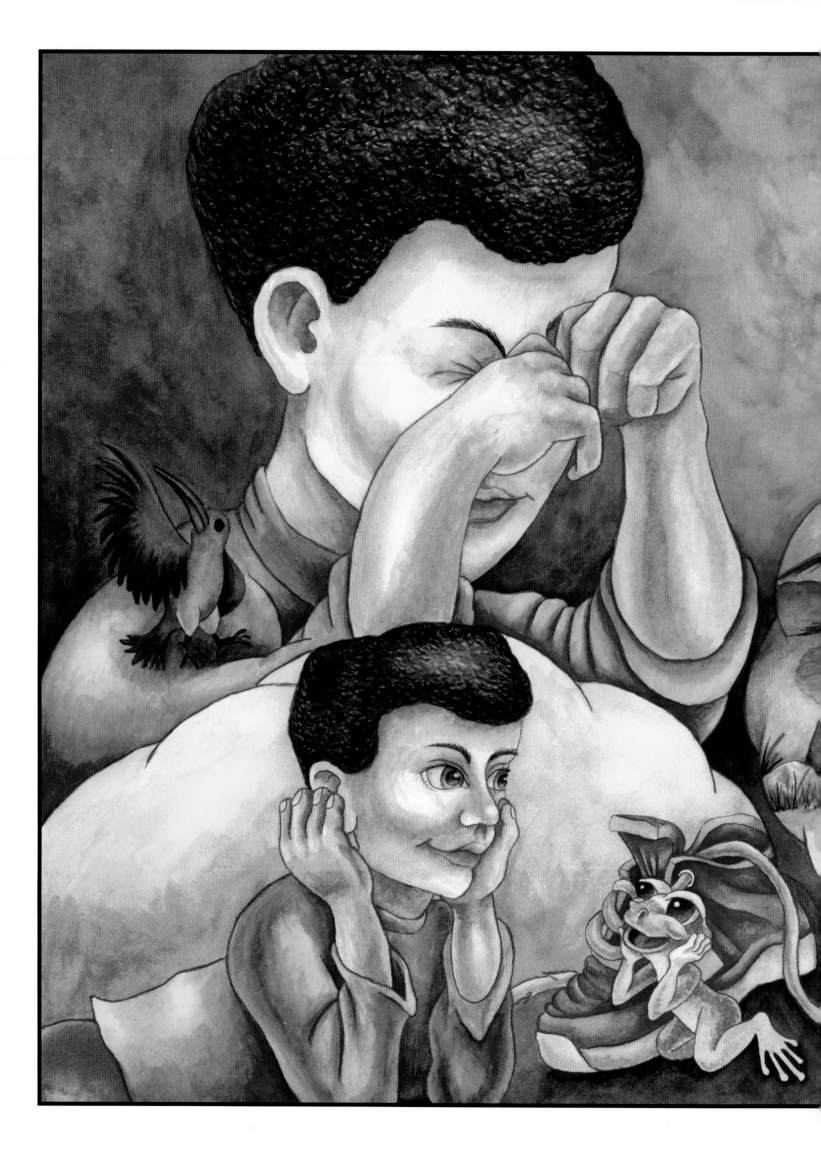

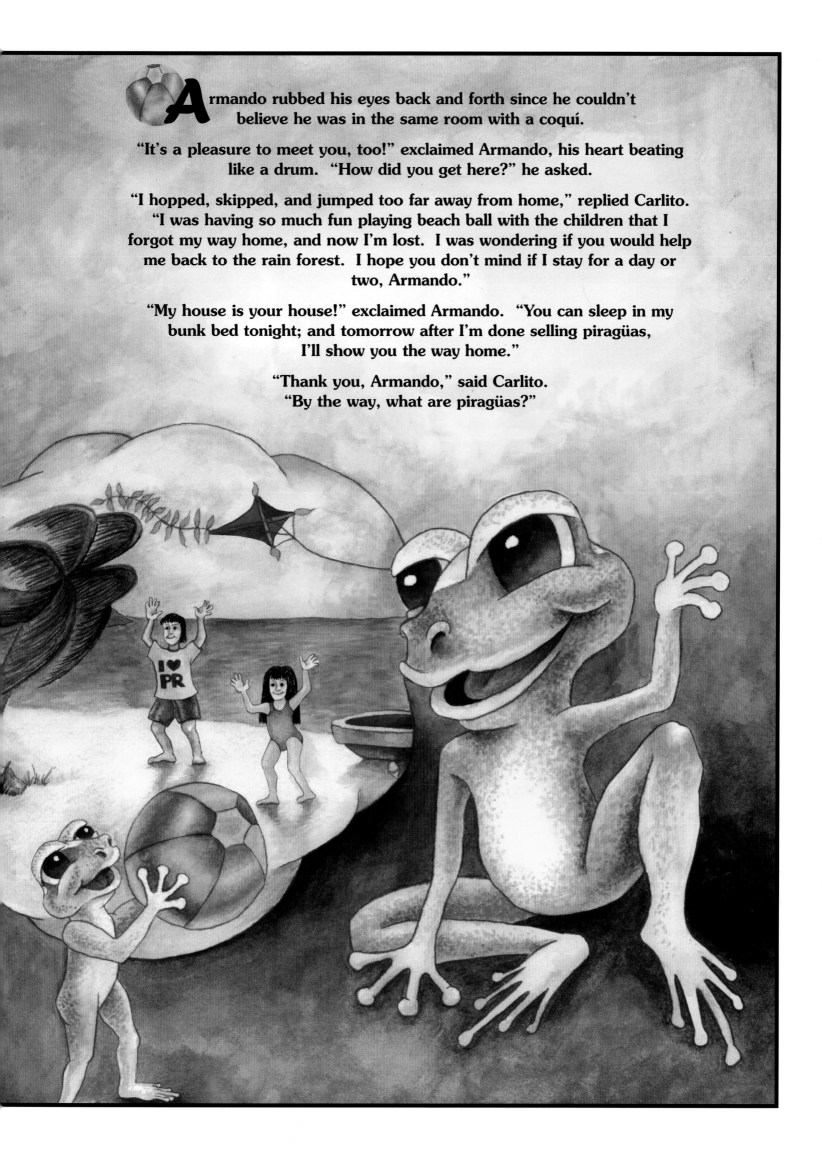

Armando rubbed his eyes back and forth since he couldn't believe he was in the same room with a coquí.

"It's a pleasure to meet you, too!" exclaimed Armando, his heart beating like a drum. "How did you get here?" he asked.

"I hopped, skipped, and jumped too far away from home," replied Carlito. "I was having so much fun playing beach ball with the children that I forgot my way home, and now I'm lost. I was wondering if you would help me back to the rain forest. I hope you don't mind if I stay for a day or two, Armando."

"My house is your house!" exclaimed Armando. "You can sleep in my bunk bed tonight; and tomorrow after I'm done selling piragüas, I'll show you the way home."

"Thank you, Armando," said Carlito. "By the way, what are piragüas?"

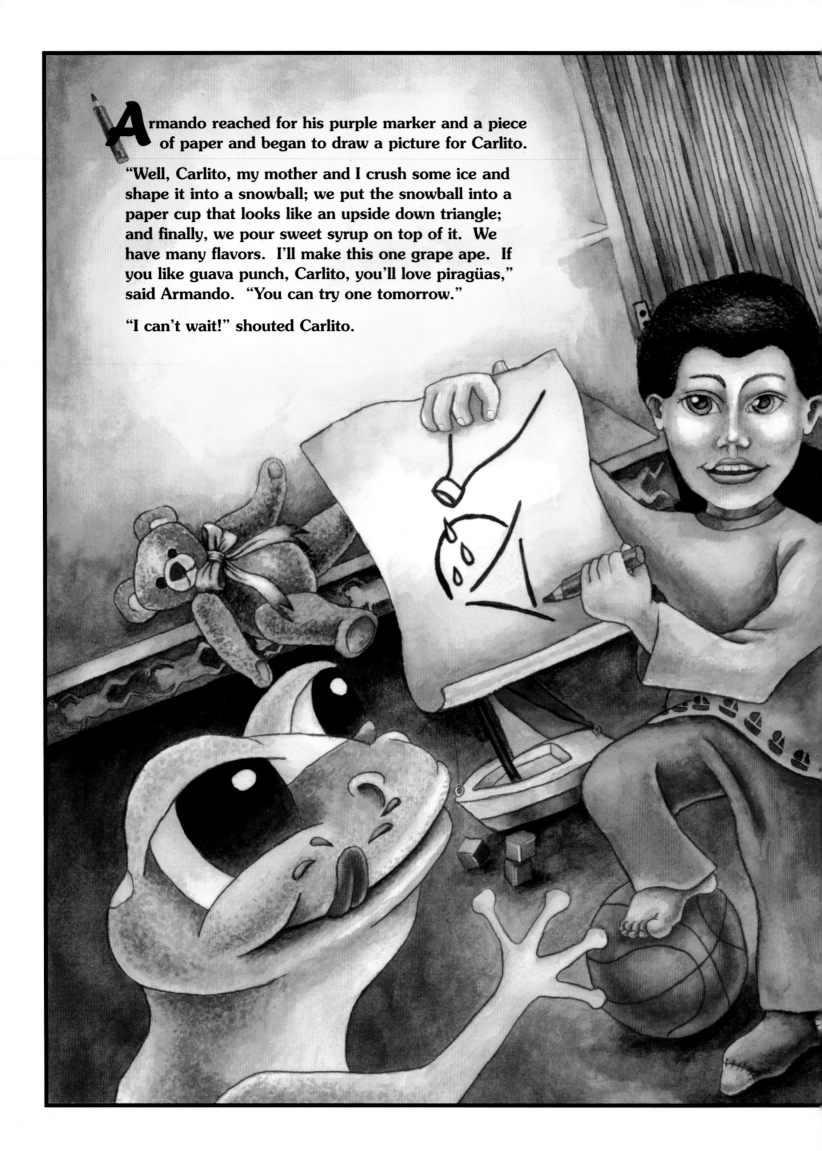

Armando reached for his purple marker and a piece of paper and began to draw a picture for Carlito.

"Well, Carlito, my mother and I crush some ice and shape it into a snowball; we put the snowball into a paper cup that looks like an upside down triangle; and finally, we pour sweet syrup on top of it. We have many flavors. I'll make this one grape ape. If you like guava punch, Carlito, you'll love piragüas," said Armando. "You can try one tomorrow."

"I can't wait!" shouted Carlito.

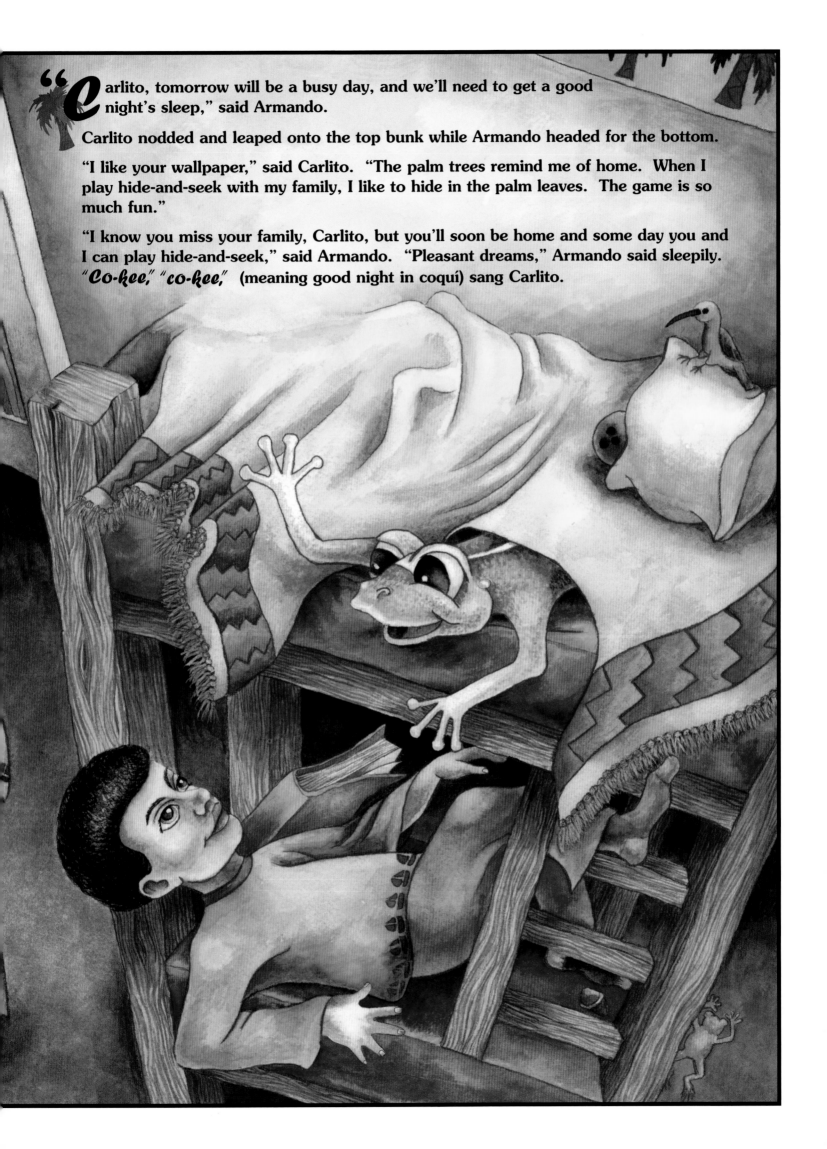

"Carlito, tomorrow will be a busy day, and we'll need to get a good night's sleep," said Armando.

Carlito nodded and leaped onto the top bunk while Armando headed for the bottom.

"I like your wallpaper," said Carlito. "The palm trees remind me of home. When I play hide-and-seek with my family, I like to hide in the palm leaves. The game is so much fun."

"I know you miss your family, Carlito, but you'll soon be home and some day you and I can play hide-and-seek," said Armando. "Pleasant dreams," Armando said sleepily. *"Co-kee," "co-kee,"* (meaning good night in coquí) sang Carlito.

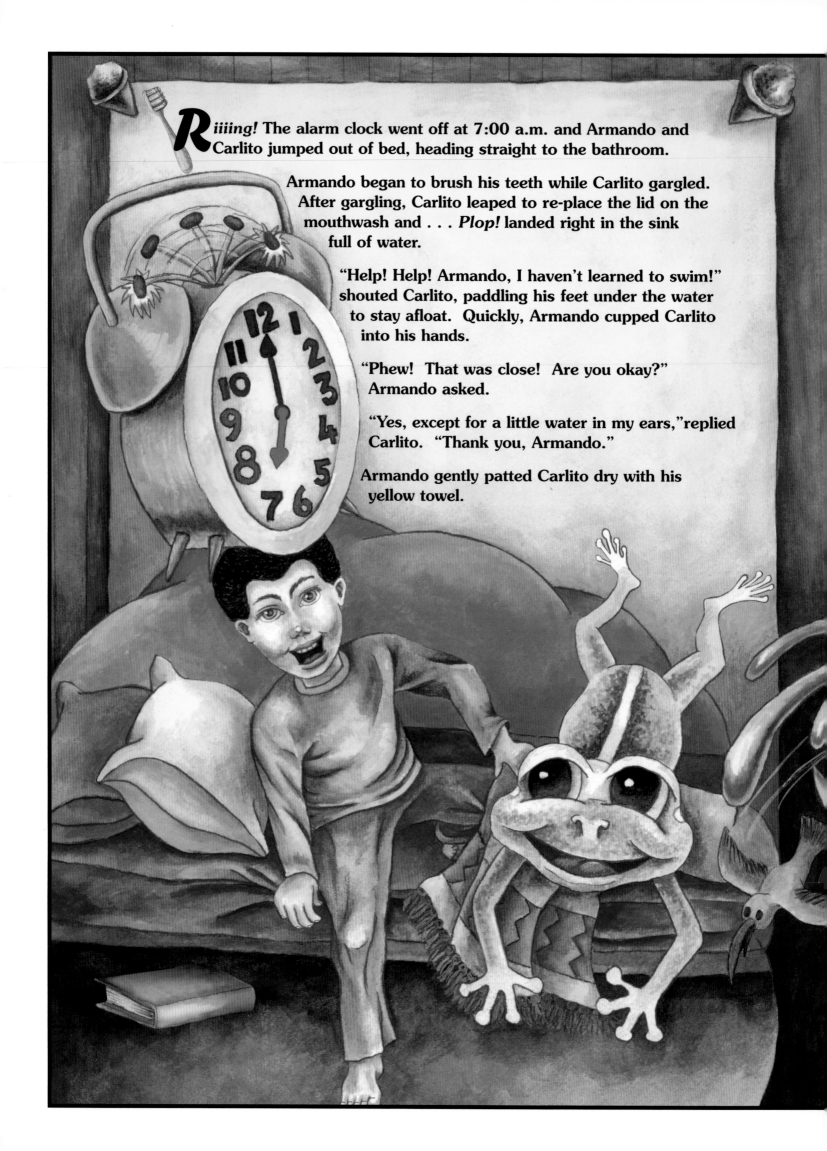

*R*iiiing! The alarm clock went off at 7:00 a.m. and Armando and Carlito jumped out of bed, heading straight to the bathroom.

Armando began to brush his teeth while Carlito gargled. After gargling, Carlito leaped to re-place the lid on the mouthwash and . . . *Plop!* landed right in the sink full of water.

"Help! Help! Armando, I haven't learned to swim!" shouted Carlito, paddling his feet under the water to stay afloat. Quickly, Armando cupped Carlito into his hands.

"Phew! That was close! Are you okay?" Armando asked.

"Yes, except for a little water in my ears," replied Carlito. "Thank you, Armando."

Armando gently patted Carlito dry with his yellow towel.

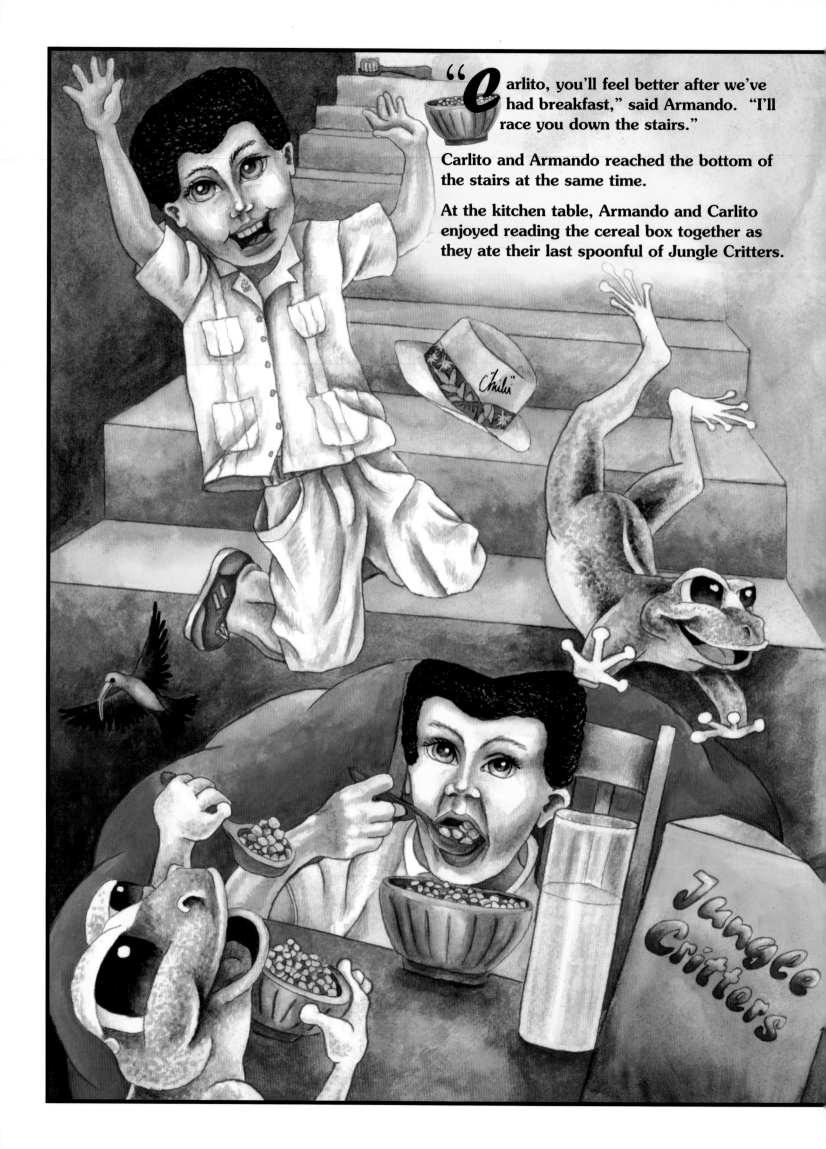

"Carlito, you'll feel better after we've had breakfast," said Armando. "I'll race you down the stairs."

Carlito and Armando reached the bottom of the stairs at the same time.

At the kitchen table, Armando and Carlito enjoyed reading the cereal box together as they ate their last spoonful of Jungle Critters.

After breakfast, Lola, Armando, and Carlito bolted outside. They stocked the piragüa pushcart with the flavored syrups, paper cups, ice, and lots of napkins. The bottled syrups looked like a bright, beautiful rainbow displayed on the cart.

Carlito eagerly jumped on Armando's shoulder waiting to start the day.

"Today we will sell many piragüas because a coquí has come into our home," said Lola.

It was a bright and sunny morning, and the tropical breeze felt good across Armando's and Lola's faces as they pushed the cart up the cobblestone streets of Old San Juan, passing wrought iron and pastel Spanish homes. The wheels of the cart rumbled, wobbled, and screeched on Calle del Cristo (Cristo Street).

Carlito noticed that
two of the flavored syrup bottles
had lost their tops and were about to spill onto the ground. Quickly, leaping
into the air, Carlito stuck his left finger into the mango tango and plugged the
raspberry blast with his right toe.

Up ahead, Carlito spotted a few of his friends in an open, horse-drawn carriage in front of the first children's museum in the Caribbean, the Museo del Niño. Excited to see Rita, José, Chi Chi, Cuban Pete, and Barbara, Carlito leaped onto the carriage giving each a mouth-watering piragüa and then waving goodbye.

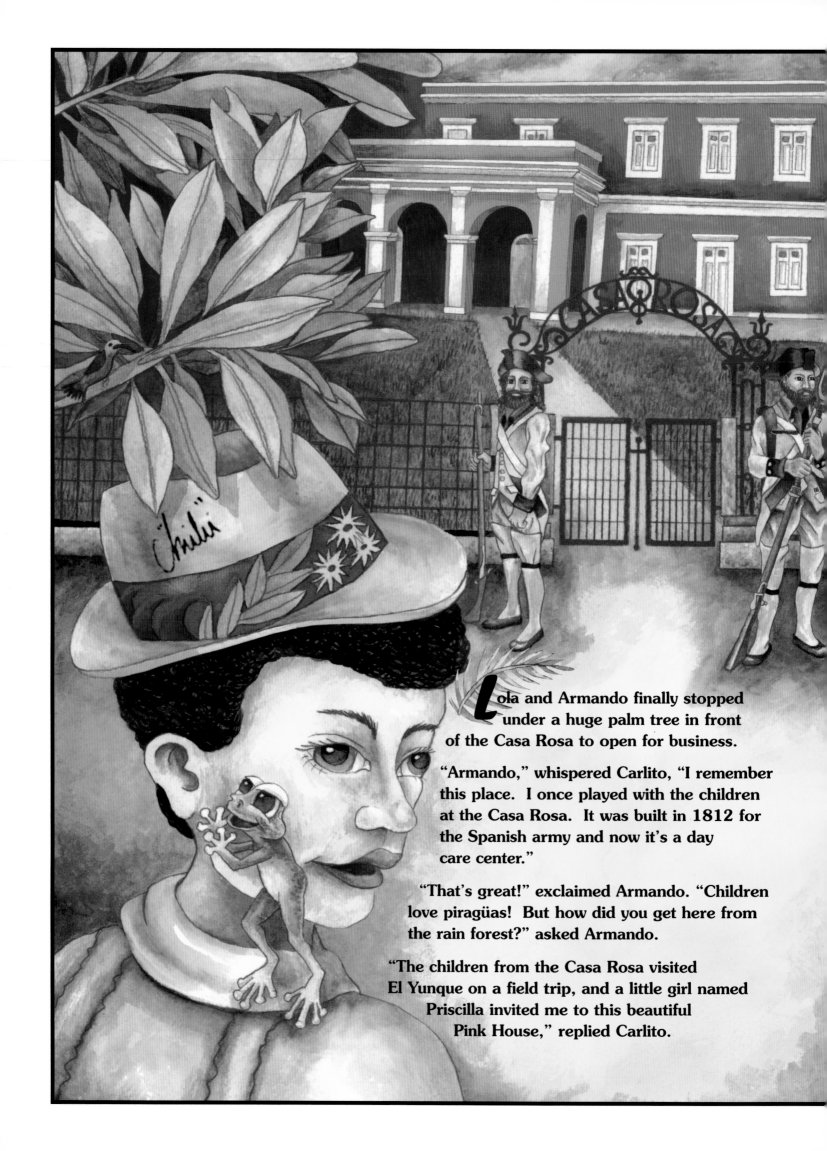

ola and Armando finally stopped under a huge palm tree in front of the Casa Rosa to open for business.

"Armando," whispered Carlito, "I remember this place. I once played with the children at the Casa Rosa. It was built in 1812 for the Spanish army and now it's a day care center."

"That's great!" exclaimed Armando. "Children love piragüas! But how did you get here from the rain forest?" asked Armando.

"The children from the Casa Rosa visited El Yunque on a field trip, and a little girl named Priscilla invited me to this beautiful Pink House," replied Carlito.

When they saw the piragüa pushcart, the Casa Rosa children, immediately, ran outside with their parents. Armando and his mother were ready for every piragüa order.

Meanwhile, someone tugged at Armando's white guayabera (gwa-yah-bera —— the traditional Puerto Rican dress shirt). Turning around, he saw a little girl with brunette hair.

"Hi! My name is Priscilla, and I thought I saw Carlito with you. We played together some time ago, and I wanted to say hello!"

"**C**arlito, it's . . ." (Armando looked on his shoulder but Carlito was gone.)

"Carlito, where are you?" asked Armando. Carlito didn't respond.

"Carlito! Carlito!" shouted Armando and his mother as they searched around the pushcart. They began to worry.

"**D**on't worry," said Priscilla. "I know where Carlito is. He likes to hide. Can you see him up there?"

"No, I can't," said Armando.

"Itsy-bitsy Carlito's not easy to find when he hides. See him now?" asked Priscilla.

"Oh, yes! Now I do!" exclaimed Armando. "He's very good at this game."

Carlito leaped down from under the huge palm tree leaf,
giving Priscilla and Armando a big hug, began to sing
"co-kee," "co-kee," "co-kee." Everyone gathered around Carlito,
eating piragüas and listening to his song about friendship:

"When you need some help or are feeling blue,
A friend is someone who can help you through,
Every day you can make friends anew,
But true, true friends are only a few."

The children and parents thanked Carlito for his
beautiful song and whistled his tune all the way home.

Armando and his mother noticed every piragüa was sold except for two. Armando was so happy that he grabbed his mother's hand and Carlito's finger and danced the plena (a folk rhythm and dance of Puerto Rico), around the pushcart.

"What flavor would you like, Carlito?" asked Armando. "There's coconut kiss and pineapple parade."

"I'll try the coconut kiss," Carlito said hungrily.

"You can eat them along the way to the rain forest," said Armando's mother.

*L*ickity, lick, lick. "*Mmmmm*! This piragüa is delicious," said Carlito, scraping the bottom of the piragüa cup with his long sticky tongue to reach the final drop of flavored syrup.

"Carlito loves Coco!"

SMACK!!! (Carlito gave Armando a big kiss on the cheek.)

"You're my true friend!" said Carlito.

"And, you're my true friend, too!" said Armando.

And off Armando went,
skipping down the
moss-covered brick road
to the rain forest, with
Carlito bouncing on
his shoulder.

As soon as they entered the rain forest, Carlito's thunderous *"CO-KEE"* call swept throughout the forest. The rain forest came alive with music. The bamboo, huge sierra palms, and giant tree ferns swayed in the wind as if waving hello.

Vita, the Puerto Rican Parrot, with her bright green and blue feathers swooshed past Carlito. She dropped a red orchid at his feet. Swirling around Armando, she landed gracefully on his shoulder and finally winked at Carlito, showing her tiny red forehead.

Peter and Petra, a pair of red, white, yellow, and green San Pedrito todies (little Saint Peter birds) perched on a vine, chirping, in glee, at the sight of Carlito, and a trio of crickets burst into a song *"¡Bienvenidos a El Yunque!"*
(Welcome to El Yunque!).

Nate, the Puerto Rican Boa, slithered out from under a rock. He danced the twist while the butterflies fanned their wings in sheer delight.

The silver colored Mountain mullet fish, singing with joy, dived in and out of the narrow waterfalls, which formed shallow pools, as the spiders crawled from under the leaves, speeding toward Carlito.

Lorenzo the Lizard raced down the waterfall's cliff, and the busy termites and beetles popped their tiny heads up from a tree bark to join the celebration.

A sky always clean
serves as a canopy.
And placid lullabies
are given by the
waves at her feet.

Carlito jumped onto a large lily pad where his mother, father, brothers, and sister were waiting for him with open arms.

"Welcome home, Carlito!" shouted his family as they gathered, merrily, around, smothering him with hugs and kisses.

Suddenly, Armando felt a raindrop on his right cheek, two on his nose, and three on his head. Opening his mouth, he caught four on his tongue, and soon a zillion drops were falling from the sky.

When at her beaches Columbus arrived, he exclaimed full of admiration,

utiful land that I seek."

Wet from head to toe, Armando paraded in the rain with the rain forest creatures. He stomped his favorite red shoes in a puddle, thinking about what a *FUN*tastic day he had with his best friend, Carlito.

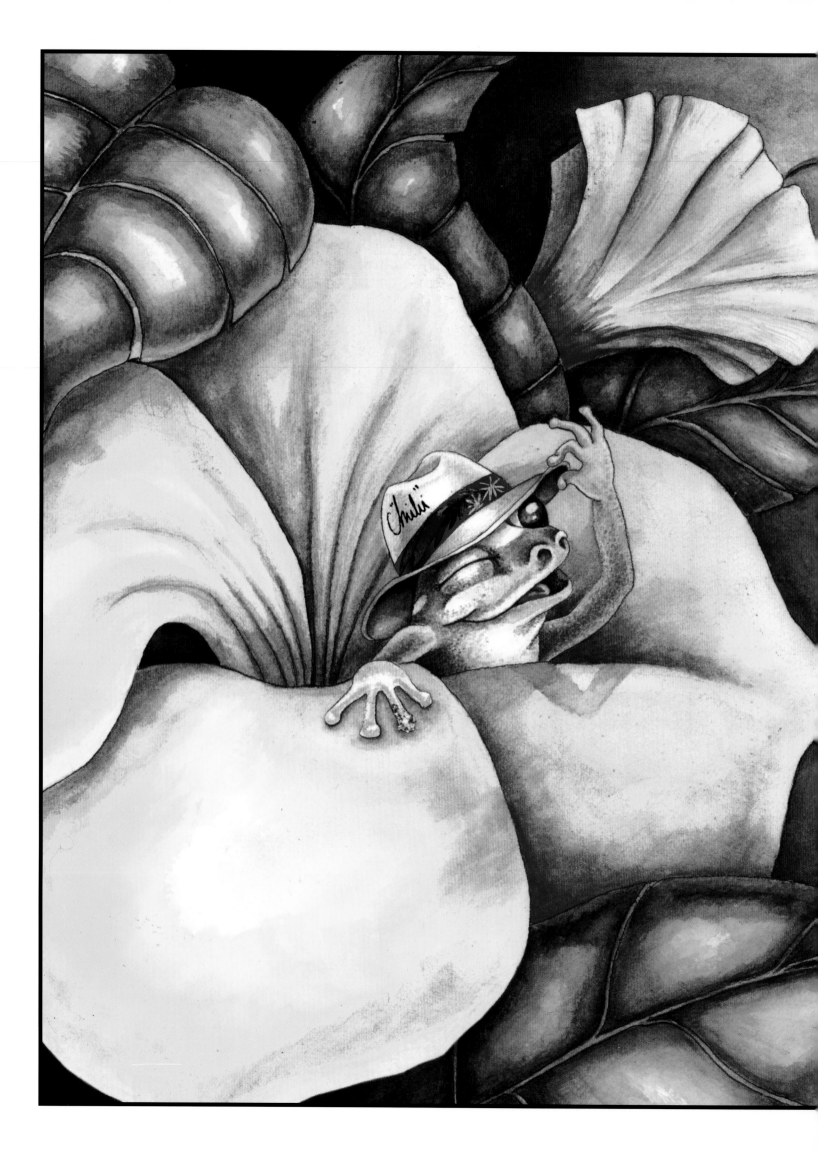

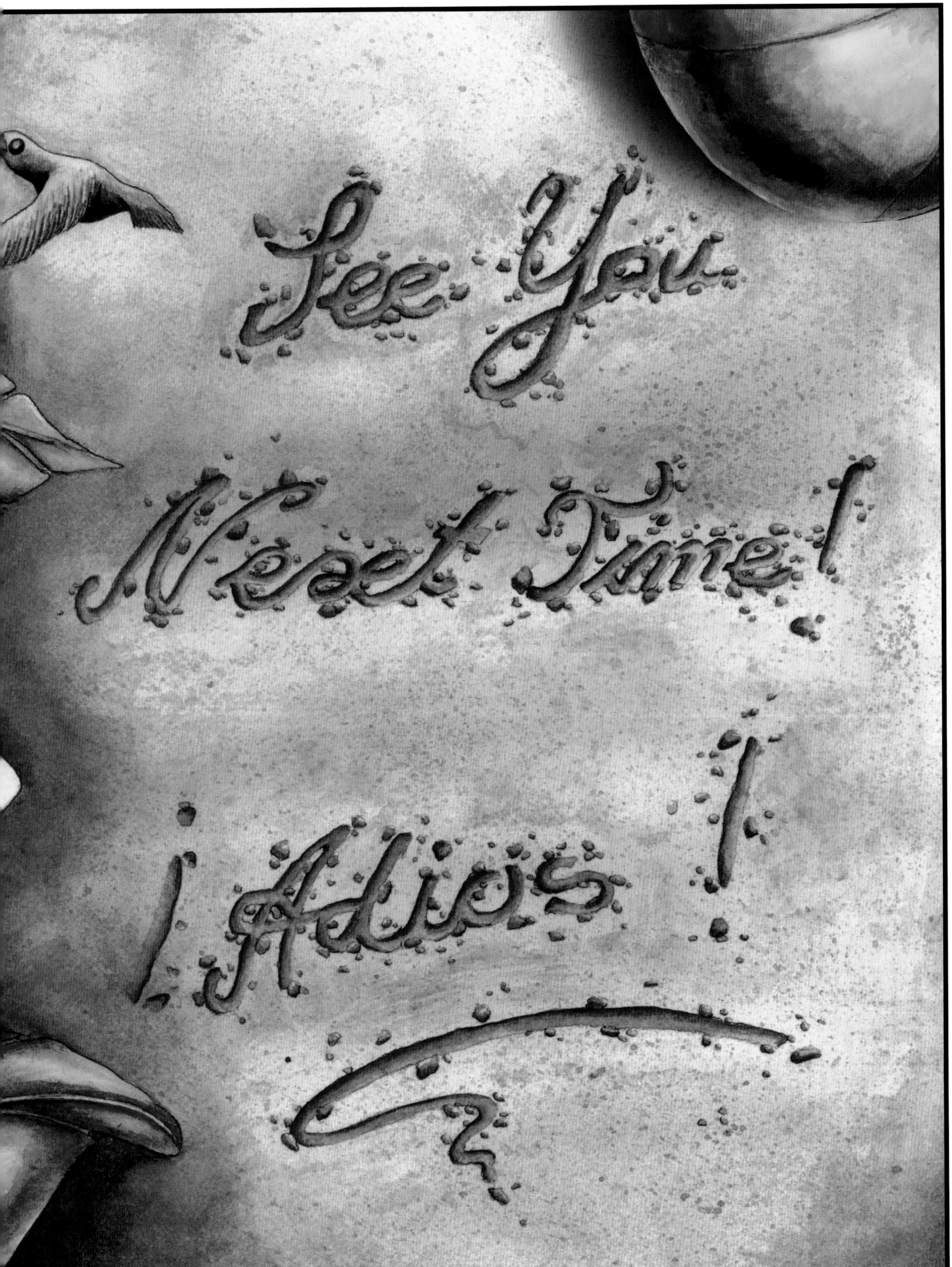
See You
Next Time!
¡Adiós!

Back Matter

FUN FACTS

A Bit of Puerto Rico History

Puerto Rico is a tropical island located between the Caribbean Sea and the North Atlantic Ocean. Puerto Rico, which means rich port, was given its name over 500 years ago by the Spanish explorers. El Morro, also known as Fort San Felipe del Morro, is Puerto Rico's best-known fortress. El Morro is the Spanish word for headland, referring to the headland on which the fort is situated. El Morro was built by the Spanish in the 1500s to prevent pirates and European enemies from entering San Juan. After the Spanish-American War, the United States claimed Puerto Rico. Puerto Rico is a Commonwealth of the United States. A Commonwealth has its own Constitution.

Splish! Splash!

El Yunque National Forest, formerly known as The Caribbean National Forest, is the only tropical rain forest in the U.S. National Forest System. More than 100 billion gallons of rainwater fall per year or 240 inches of rain per year. There are almost 50 types of orchid flowers that grow here. The Puerto Rican Parrot *(Amazona vittata)* makes its home in the forest. It is about 12 inches long and it is one of the 10 most endangered species (types) of birds in the world. Presently the population consists of approximately 47 birds. The Puerto Rican Boa *(Epicrates inornatus)* is also an endangered species. It can reach up to 6 feet long. The silver colored dajao or Mountain mullet fish *(Agonostomus monticola)* is well known in the forest. It fills the same ecological niche as trout in the United States. The San Pedrito Tody or Little Saint Peter *(Todus mexicanus)* is a small bird about the size of a hummingbird seen mostly in pairs. The Yokahú Observation Tower, which is located in the rain forest, offers panoramic views of El Yunque.

Oooooh, Pretty

The Flor de Maga or Flower of Maga is Puerto Rico's national flower. It grows on the Maga tree and it is native to Puerto Rico. It is a large red tropical flower.

Want to Dance?

One of the most popular styles of folk music and dance on the island is the Plena. The instruments used in the Plena are the plenera drums (handheld and lightweight drums usually in small, medium, and large sizes), the güiro (gwee-roh) (a dried out gourd with grooves cut into it that is rubbed with a scraper or stick), the panderos (tambourine-like instrument), and the cuatro (a guitar-like instrument having five double strings and tuned in fourths).

The *Eleutherodactylus coqui* likes to come out and play on rainy days, cloudy days, and at night. When the coqui sings "co" it is warning other males to leave, and when it sings "qui" it is calling and welcoming the female coqui to reproductive activity. For the female coqui frog this means "I love you!" Only the male coquies call during courtship. The *Eleutherodactylus coqui* is also known as Common Coqui because it can be found in the rain forest and throughout the island of Puerto Rico. For instance, it is a species that is commonly seen resting on the walls of buildings and homes. As the name indicates, free fingers, the *Eleutherodactylus coqui* has no interdigital membranes, which could indicate they are not adapted to swim. Coqui frogs have five digits in the rear and four digits in front. The coquies are vital to the food chain and are the most important nocturnal (night) predator on the island. There are so many variations in markings in the species *Eleutherodactylus coqui* that they can easily be mistaken as different species, and its color is light tan to brown.

The smallest of the Puerto Rican coquí species is the Elfin Coqui and the largest is the Webbed Coqui. The Webbed Coqui is the only species that has webbed feet. The Puerto Rican coquies range in size from approximately 0.6 inches to 3.1 inches. The females are larger than the males.

The coquies do not have their babies over water nor do they pass through a tadpole stage. Some of the coquí species fertilize their eggs internally, and once they are laid, the father protects the eggs by lying on them to keep them moist. The Golden Coqui is the only species that is ovoviviparous, which means that the female keeps the eggs in her oviducts where they develop and are delivered fully born. Some coquí frogs can fit into the smallest places like a teaspoon — how cute!

There are 17 coquí species native to Puerto Rico and each species has its own unique song. Presently, six species of coquies are threatened or in danger of extinction as the result of deforestation, hurricanes, and pollution: the Golden Coqui, Eneida's Coqui, Webbed Coqui, Martillito Coqui, Caoba Coqui, and Guajon Coqui. The coquí is Puerto Rico's island mascot.

The 17 Species of Puerto Rican Coquies

Common Name:	Spanish Name:	Scientific Name:	Found:
Common Coqui	coquí común	*Eleutherodactylus coqui*	In highlands & lowlands
Churi Coqui (a/k/a Red-eyed Coqui)	coquí churí	*Eleutherodactylus antillensis*	In lowlands
Guajon Coqui	coquí guajón or demonio	*Eleutherodactylus cooki*	In caves
Cricket Coqui (a/k/a Green Coqui)	coquí grillo	*Eleutherodactylus gryllus*	In bromeliads
Shrub Coqui (a/k/a Grass Coqui)	coquí de las hierbas	*Eleutherodactylus brittoni*	In grasses - in highlands & lowlands
Whistling Coqui (a/k/a Cochran's Treefrog)	coquí pitito	*Eleutherodactylus cochranae*	In dry places & lowlands
Elfin Coqui (a/k/a Dwarf Coqui)	coquí duende	*Eleutherodactylus unicolor*	In mountain range of Luquillo, (in under-growth & roots of Dwarf Forest)
Golden Coqui	coquí dorado	*Eleutherodactylus jasperi*	In bromeliads
Hedrick's Coqui (a/k/a Treehole Coqui)	coquí de hedrick	*Eleutherodactylus hedricki*	In tree trunks
Melodious Coqui	coquí melodioso	*Eleutherodactylus weightmanae*	On ground base
Mona's Coqui	coquí de mona	*Eleutherodactylus monensis*	On island of Mona
Mountain Coqui (a/k/a Upland Coqui)	coquí de la montaña	*Eleutherodactylus portoricensis*	In highlands
Webbed Coqui	coquí palmeado	*Eleutherodactylus karlschmidti*	On the shores, mountain streams, near rocks where water splashes
Eneida's Coqui (a/k/a Elegant Coqui)	coquí de eneida	*Eleutherodactylus eneidae*	In highlands
Caoba Coqui (a/k/a Richmond's Coqui)	coquí caoba	*Eleutherodactylus richmondi*	In highlands
Martillito Coqui (a/k/a Locust Coqui)	coquí martillito	*Eleutherodactylus locustus*	In highlands
Juan A. Rivero's Coqui	coquí de juan rivero	*Eleutherodactylus juanriveroi*	In a fresh water wetland in Toa Baja

Classification:

Kingdom	Group	Order	Family	Genus	Species
Animal	Amphibian	Anura	Leptodactylidae	Eleutherodactylus	Coqui

References:

Joglar, Rafael L., 1998. *Los Coquíes de Puerto Rico*. Editorial de la Universidad de Puerto Rico, San Juan, Puerto Rico.

Joglar, Rafael L., 1999. *¡Que cante el Coquí! Ensayos, Cartas y otros documentos sobre la conservación de la Biodiversidad en Puerto Rico (1987-1999)* Proyecto Coquí. San Juan, Puerto Rico.

Proyecto Coquí: www.coqui.uprr.pr/esp/index.html.

U.S. Fish & Wildlife Service: www.fws.gov.

Stanzas of Puerto Rico's national anthem, La Borinqueña, have been mentioned throughout the story.

La Borinqueña-Music by Felix Astol Artés and words by Manuel Fernández Juncos.

Many Thanks!

I extend, wholeheartedly, my appreciation and sincere thanks to those who took time out of their busy schedule to review the manuscript entitled *There's a Coquí in My Shoe!* as well as provide their endorsements to the story. In addition, I would like to thank Rita Moreno, José Feliciano, Juan "Chi Chi" Rodríguez, Pedro "Cuban Pete" Aguilar, and his dancing partner, Barbara Craddock, and Dr. Rafael L. Joglar (of the University of Puerto Rico), who gave permission to be illustrated in *There's a Coquí in My Shoe!*

In this book, one of my many objectives was to incorporate an illustration (the horse-drawn carriage scene) depicting Puerto Rican celebrities that have made, and continue to make, a positive impact on the Puerto Rican community and around the world. I greatly admire and respect Rita Moreno, José Feliciano, Juan "Chi Chi" Rodríguez, and Pedro "Cuban Pete" Aguilar. The positioning of Ms. Moreno at the forefront of the carriage, holding the reins, symbolizes how this "amazing" woman has paved the way for Latina actresses today. The three distinguished gentlemen seated in the carriage are champions in the Hispanic community and superb male role models for children today. "Cuban Pete" is shown wearing his first dance costume and a reproduction of this costume is a permanent part of the RAICES Latin Music Museum's collection. The museum is located in New York City. These celebrities are excellent examples of individuals who held onto their dreams despite many obstacles encountered in their lives. It is my hope that children everywhere will reach and hold onto their dreams just like they did.

I would also like to thank Dr. Rafael L. Joglar, the leading authority on the *Eleutherodactylus coqui* and other Puerto Rican coquí species. I congratulate him for his 30 years of researching these elusive frogs, and I thank him for his expert advice regarding the correct colorings and markings of these amphibians. The accuracy of the 17 species of coquíes mentioned in this book would not be possible without his research and consultation. Bravo, Dr. Joglar!

Also, I extend my thanks to the Puerto Rico Tourism Company for its assistance regarding the Luquillo Beach scene. Luquillo Beach, which is near El Yunque National Forest, is Puerto Rico's most famous beach. There are facilities for the handicapped that include a ramp into the sea and wheel chairs, with large wheels, for sand and sea. This gives handicapped individuals an opportunity to experience and enjoy the calm waters at this beach. The program is called "Sea Without Barriers" Program. I would also like to thank Héctor Cardona, President of the Puerto Rico Olympic Committee, for his permission to allow me to illustrate the 2002 Puerto Rico Olympic Coquí Pin. My heartfelt thanks to professional dancer and competition judge Barbara Craddock for her assistance. Ms. Craddock, along with "Cuban Pete," were the only dancers invited to perform at the Tito Puente Tribute. A special thanks to Juan "Chi Chi" Rodríguez and his manager, Eric McClenaghan, for their permission to allow me to illustrate Mr. Rodríguez's signature white fedora prior to Mr. Rodríguez's involvement in publishing *There's a Coquí in My Shoe!*

Marisa

Acknowledgment for PROYECTO COQUÍ, THE CENTER FOR BIOLOGICAL DIVERSITY, MAUNABO DEVELOPMENT COMMITTEE, and YO LIMPIO A PUERTO RICO

The threatened and/or in danger of extinction scene would not be possible without the help of certain organizations and educational programs. The following resources were instrumental for the author's completion of this scene:

 Proyecto Coquí, an organization in which one of its many goals is to develop a program of environmental education to orient and exhort the public to a more active participation in the protection and conservation of our wildlife and areas of ecological importance;

 The Center for Biological Diversity, a science-based environmental advocacy organization that works to protect endangered species and wild places throughout the world through science, advocacy, education, and environmental law. Since 1984 The Center has been successful in obtaining Endangered Species Act (ESA) protection for over 329 species. The Center is headquartered in Tucson, Arizona;

 The Maunabo Development Committee, a citizen's group that works on coastal and wildlife protection and environmental education, which is based in Maunabo in Southeast Puerto Rico; and

 Yo Limpio a Puerto Rico (President and Founder Ignacio Barsottelli), an educational program dedicated to creating awareness and caring for the environment in Puerto Rico. Some of "Yo Limpio's" yearly clean up volunteers include the Cub Scouts, Brownie Scouts, and older levels of scouts.

The author extends her deepest thanks to the above organizations and educational programs for their kind assistance in this project!

"A truly lovely story that should be enjoyed by children of all ethnic backgrounds."— **Rita Moreno**
(The first Hispanic performer to win all four of the most prestigious show business awards: 1962 Oscar for West Side Story, Emmy for The Muppets & Rockford Files, Tony for The Ritz on Broadway, Grammy for the Electric Company album, etc.).

"Inspiring! A story that children everywhere will enjoy!" — **Juan "Chi Chi" Rodríguez**
(Professional Golfer, 22 Senior PGA Tour wins & 8 regular PGA Tour wins, Herb Graffis and Bob Jones Awards, Inductee into the World Sports Humanitarian Hall of Fame and Golf Hall of Fame in United States and Puerto Rico, Founder of the Chi Chi Rodríguez Youth Foundation, etc.).

"A charming little story. Thank you for the opportunity to share it with our children."
— **Mr. and Mrs. José Feliciano** (José Feliciano is acclaimed as the greatest living guitarist, awarded over 45 Gold & Platinum records, won 16 Grammy nominations & 6 Grammy Awards, best known all over the world for his song Feliz Navidad, etc.).

"A captivating tale sure to please children everywhere!"— **Pedro "Cuban Pete" Aguilar**
(Puerto Rican Mambo Master, Latin dancer recognized in the Latin Jazz Exhibit, Smithsonian Institute, Washington, D.C., consultant and choreographer to the hit movie Mambo Kings teaching Armand Assanti and Antonio Banderas how to dance. Given the nickname "Cuban Pete" after Desi Arnaz's song "CUBAN PETE, King of the Latin Beat." Command performance for Queen Elizabeth, The Queen Mother of England, two White House performances for Presidents Eisenhower and Johnson, performance at Madison Square Garden for Prime Minister Ben Gurion of Israel, featured in Life Magazine (12/20/54), etc.).

"It is an amazing story for children all over the world to learn about the Puerto Rican "coquí" and other cultural insights of the island. The story also fosters friends and family values which describe our Puerto Rican society."
— **Nancy Velázquez, English Program Director, Commonwealth of Puerto Rico Department of Education.**

"What a delightful story! This is a story that all children will love!"
— **The Honorable Carlos Vizcarrondo Irizarry,**
Former Speaker of the Puerto Rican House of Representatives, San Juan, Puerto Rico.

"I enjoyed reading and sharing this story with my children. I am sure many children around the world will love it, as my children did." — **José Fuertes, President of Coco Rico International.**

"There's a Coquí in My Shoe! is a gem of a story that will undoubtedly appeal to children everywhere."
— **Robert L. Walton, M.D., Chief of Plastic & Reconstructive Surgery, University of Chicago Hospital.**
(Dr. Walton was honored at La Fortaleza (the Governor's mansion) for coming to Puerto Rico several times a year for 16 years to operate on children with deformities).

"There should be a "coquí" in every child's shoe. Congratulations!"
— **Héctor Cardona, President of Puerto Rico National Olympic Committee.**

"I congratulate you for writing this story. It is time that we have literature that is refreshing and culturally relevant."— **Carmen L. Vega,**
Executive Director/Founder of Museo del Niño (Children's Museum) in San Juan, Puerto Rico.

"What a delightful story for children. I can just imagine the bright, cheerful colors that the illustrator will use in the pictures to go along with the story. It is wonderful that your story has a great deal of information for all children but Puerto Rican children, in particular, need to see their heritage in books. With our growing Latino population, this book will have a niche on our shelves and a place in our hearts." — **Dr. J. Robert Dornish, Professor Emeritus, Kutztown University, Kutztown, Pennsylvania.**
(teacher of children's literature at the graduate and undergraduate levels for 28 years).

"Thank you for giving a piece of our culture to children abroad. Carlito the Coquí is looking forward to giving all your readers a free concert in his unique way. It is a beautiful story!" – **Luis E. Rodríguez-Rivera, Former Secretary, Department of Natural and Environmental Resources, San Juan, Puerto Rico.**

"This story opens the doors to Puerto Rican children in the United States to enter into the world of environmental conservation. Also, this magisterial and impressionist story presents a cultural vision about Puerto Rican heritage and breaks down the walls of language and presents to the Anglo-American children Puerto Rico's natural resources. The natural has no boundaries; the world is our home and is property of all. By this reason, this story presents to our best people, the children, the opportunity to relate and experience this amazing species. The Puerto Rican coquí is more than just a frog; this species represents part of the soul and the identity of our country. The conservation of the coquí and its habitats is the goal to preserve this species forever. This storybook offers to the Boriñquen children a unique opportunity to make an imaginative travel into the history, science, and ecology of Puerto Rico and makes a Puerto Rican cultural contribution. This story is a very important contribution of the author to the constellation of the American literature. The big changes in society begin with little changes, step-by-step. This book also presents to the American society a beautiful contribution of Latin authors to enrich the nation."
— **Dr. Pedro M. Torres Morales, Chairman, Maunabo Development Committee, Maunabo, Puerto Rico.**

"A delightful story that paints a picture of the flora and fauna of the Puerto Rican rain forest, full of color and animation. Children can easily picture in their minds the insects, birds, trees, plants, and other animals. The sequence in Old San Juan is also lively and fun . . . one becomes easily interested in this story about a little boy and the coquí that he discovers in his shoe."
— **Jorge A. Santini Padilla, Mayor of the City of San Juan, Puerto Rico.**

"What a beautiful story! For me it was especially touching since the Liberty High School Orchestra just returned from Puerto Rico. We stayed in Fajardo and visited the rain forest on two occasions. The sounds of the coquí were absolutely mesmerizing! Your story is a wonderful way to share one of the many natural beauties of the island. You should consider doing an entire series of stories!"
— **William J. Burkhardt, Former Principal of Liberty High School, Bethlehem, Pennsylvania.**

"Your story brought joy to my heart. As I read, I felt transported to Old San Juan where in a cobblestone street I savored a coconut kiss piragüa with Carlito and Armando playing by my side. You have a gift and zest for writing, and I can't wait to see what the illustrator does with your vibrant, colorful scenes. By the way, I shared the manuscript with my high school students as a way of encouraging would-be writers. Thank you for sharing your gift of writing! Adelante!"
— **Nerida Cruz-Vélez, ESL Teacher at Bartlett High School, Elgin, Illinois.**

"A wonderful story for young children. The theme of friendship and the introduction to the beautiful Puerto Rico culture both teaches and entertains. Coquí will be loved by all children."
— **Alice Dornish, Professor Emeritus, Bethlehem, Pennsylvania.**

"There's a Coquí in My Shoe! is an absolute masterpiece of a children's book. I have read the text to my nieces and nephews, several times, and each time I see them they want to hear it again! Combining an exciting story with so much well-researched information about the magical coquíes of Puerto Rico makes for one super heart-warming, uplifting, awesome book!"
— **Peter Galvin, Legal Director, The Center for Biological Diversity, Garberville, California.**